DEATH WITH DIGNITY

A story

J. LEE PORTER

ED TEJA

nomadicgiant.com

ISBN: 978-1-949063-16-5

AUTHORS' NOTE

This story is fiction, although it is true that Thailand can follow people home, or wherever else they go. In our case, a meetup at Elephant Bay, on Koh Chang Island, where we were soaked in Thai whisky, relaxed by massages, and embroiled in the chaos and pageantry of Muay Thai matches, we came up with this story. And now it follows us everywhere.

"In the meantime, let our souls kiss and my faith and true love shall never fail to assure thee that though fortune hath not given you a rich and powerful man yet God hath bestowed on you one that will live and die."

— Endymion Porter

I stood at the buffet at the hotel, staring numbly at a bewildering array of food. So much of it was strange, exotic, and, for me, a little unsettling. I suppose it wasn't exotic for the place. After all, I was in Bangkok, Thailand, trying to sort out breakfast on a gorgeous morning.

Some of the offerings… well, I wasn't even sure what they were. Bowls overflowed with strange, prickly, bright-colored fruits (even purple) and porridge dishes arranged with bowls overflowing with odd bits of things (seaweed?) that seemed to be condiments. There was an orange juice, labeled 'blood orange juice' that did look disconcertingly like blood.

Looking at it all made me shudder. I want my breakfast to be comforting, not an adventure or some grand experiment. All that choice and strangeness made my stomach tense.

Fortunately, the hotel also offered an entire table of more familiar offerings. As I heaped my plate high with scrambled eggs and bacon, rolls, and potatoes, I thanked my lucky stars that I'd insisted we stay at a five-star hotel. When we arranged the trip, Jake had tried to talk me into letting him book us into a local hotel.

"It would give us a chance to experience something more like the real thing—the real Asia," he said.

That kind of experience, being immersed in an entirely new world, a different culture, sounded dreadful. The only exotic experience I wanted was one that would make me, a rather finicky and particular Westerner, comfortable while away from home. Despite the higher cost, I'd insisted on staying at the Marriott. "I want clean, white sheets on the bed, well-appointed rooms, and familiar food," I told him. And I'd gotten it, even if a lot of unfamiliar food was along for the ride.

As I turned and headed for a table, Jake staggered into the dining room, looking the worse for wear.

"Hey, sleepy head," I teased.

"Right," he said. "One hell of night."

"That's one way to describe it," I said.

The day before, we'd met with an Australian businessman named Ralph. After discussing business, he had insisted on showing us the town. As his notion of entertainment meant a tour of sleazy bars and nightlife, and as much as Jake had drunk, seeing him up and about this early surprised me.

"You could've slept in. Our flight back home isn't until early this afternoon, and the hotel isn't even 20 miles from the airport."

He sat down, looking at me oddly. "Typical that you'd know that and not much else about Bangkok."

"The distance to the airport is important," I said, once again struck with Jake's knack for making me feel defensive for using common sense.

He didn't hear me. His attention had shifted to the important task of waving an empty cup at a waiter patrolling the dining room with a silver coffeepot. "Help," he said. "Desperate man here."

The man smiled and came over to fill his cup. "Bless you," Jake said, taking a deep swallow, then shaking his head. "I have bad news."

"News? You just got up."

"From last night. Seems I lost my passport."

His odd grin made me wonder if he was teasing me. "Don't make a joke like that."

"It's not a joke."

"How did you manage to lose it?"

"The way a person loses things. You put it down somewhere and forget about it." He cocked his head. "In this case, I'm pretty sure I left it in the taxi that brought us home last night."

"What makes you think that?"

He shrugged. "Because I'm sure that's where I left my jacket, and I had my passport in the pocket. *Quid erat* something or other, as the Romans are supposed to have said." He squinted. "Last night I spent an hour tearing my room apart, and it isn't there."

"What do we do now?"

He stole one of my rolls and nibbled it. "Eating breakfast comes to mind. And then... you didn't happen to write down the number of the taxi, did you?"

"No. Why would I? I barely remembered the taxi ride." I'd been too worried that the taxi was taking us to the wrong hotel.

"Because you do shit like that. You keep every damn receipt and write down all sorts of things."

"For tax purposes."

"Whatever." He waved a hand. "It was worth asking."

"I wasn't in top form. It was late."

"Past your bedtime."

"I was tired, and you were drunk."

He sighed. "So, even if that's where it is, safe in some taxi, we can't get it. Now, all that matters is that I don't have a passport. Happily, I have my wallet, and I have a photocopy of my passport tucked away in it."

"You can't fly home with a photocopy," I said. My stomach was tighter now than when thinking about the strange food. Even the eggs and bacon smelled wrong.

"But it will simplify getting a new one."

"What the hell do we do? That's an official document and you can't fly without one."

"We? You are good to go. Best thing is, you stick to the plan. Catch the plane back to California and take care of business."

"And leave you here?"

"I talked to the airline this morning, and I can reschedule the flight for a small fee. No big deal. I called the embassy this morning and learned from their recorded message that I need to show up at their doorstep at 9am Monday morning."

"You want me to leave you?"

"I have to do a bunch of paperwork, but once I do, they will issue me an emergency passport. I think the gist of their message was: 'Don't go home without one.'" He laughed.

"That sucks," I said.

"I screwed up. It isn't such a big deal," he said, reaching over to steal a piece of bacon from my plate. "It's all fixable. Just a glitch. I know you hate glitches, but shit happens." He pointed a finger at my plate and made a face. "You do know you are in Asia, right? The food here is incredible."

"I like bacon."

"They've got stuff here that you'll never see at home. To learn about it, you actually have to eat it."

"You seem to be enjoying my bacon well enough." His criticism made me snarky.

"I'm starving. When I finish my coffee, I'll wander over and get some stir fry and other delicacies. This is to hold me over. It would be poor form to starve to death on the trek to the buffet table. The hotel management would not approve."

I watched him, wondering how he could take the idea of losing his passport so calmly. "Why is it that I'm more upset about this than you? You losing your passport, I mean."

That got me another laugh. "Because you always get upset when anything changes or makes you alter your plans. You don't like things that take you out of your comfort zone."

"And you do?"

"Not always, but in this case, I see it as an unplanned adventure. That's why your job in the company is to make sure the plans work out and mine is to bring in the business."

That was true. Jake was the idea man—the big picture guy who sold his vision to clients. We were partners in San Mateo Sparkle; we ran teams that cleaned high-end homes and offices. Well, I ran it. While Jake helped clients decide it was a grand idea to pay us high fees to have their places reliably cleaned to perfection, I dealt with the gritty detail. I pulled the resources together, arranging things to make it happen.

Even after years of working together, I'd never understood Jake's cavalier attitude about things going wrong. It didn't bother him. "You lost an important document. That was careless of you."

"Yup, it was. But, c'mon, Billy boy. Lighten up. The way I see it, that means I have to extend my trip a few days. That's not a disaster. The sinking of the Titanic, or whatever ship actually sank… now there was a disaster. But no lives will be lost correcting my mistake. I'll shell out a few bucks and while I wait for the bureaucrats to do their thing, I'll see a little of Thailand. I'd love to go to the floating markets."

I'd read about them in the guidebook and stared at the pictures. "Why go to such unsanitary places? They do have supermarkets here."

He laughed at me, raising my hackles. I wondered if Jake was telling me the truth. He'd wanted to make this a ten-day trip, but I'd insisted we keep it short. "We only need to be there long enough to meet with this Ralph and hear his pitch," I'd said.

And that's what happened. Ralph had a manufacturing business and wanted investors for expansion. After meeting him, he gave us a tour of the facilities. Then he'd taken us out. By that time, I'd learned more than enough. I wanted no part of Ralph's enterprise and I was ready to go home.

"Unsanitary?" Jake was laughing. "That's become your favorite word for everything here. It's what you said about the place we went to watch the show last night."

The memory of the crowded night market, ringed with sex shows made me cringe. "Please never mention that back in the US. If Doreen knew that we'd let your creepy Australian pal take us to one of those, I'd never hear the end of it."

"My creepy pal? Ralph is a businessman who wants us to invest. He was entertaining us in the local style."

"It was disgusting."

Jake shrugged. "The eye of the beholder and all that. Besides, you can blame it on me. Doreen knows I'm a bad influence."

"And that so-called business of his?"

"I know you are uncomfortable with the idea."

"Not just the idea, it's the place itself."

He shrugged. "It's a business."

"And I don't see how we could manage the operation from California."

"We wouldn't. Ralph has been running the manufacturing operation fine without our help for several years. All he wants is someone to fund his expansion and help find new clients that want to subcontract toy manufacturing."

"And it's a dump—a sweatshop."

"He complies with all the local regulations that he can't bribe people to ignore."

"That's no answer!"

He grinned, letting me know that he brought up the issue of bribery to taunt me. Jake considered my attitudes puritanical.

"So tell me how we would keep an eye on things from halfway around the world? We couldn't even be sure he kept honest books."

"He's honest."

"You just said he bribes officials."

That earned me another cavalier shrug. "That's the way business is done here."

"Which is a good reason for not doing business here," I said. "Besides, neither of us knows the first thing about manufacturing. We run a service company."

Jake just grinned. "You make problems where there are none. Shit, subcontracting is a service business every bit as much as what we do. And when it comes to manufacturing, Ralph knows what he is doing. We'd be investing in a profitable, ongoing operation."

"But why do that in Asia?"

Jake gave me an incredulous look. "Why? Because that's where this opportunity is. We can't invest in his manufacturing operation in San Jose because he doesn't have any there. US companies subcontract to low-cost Asian operations. An outfit in San Jose couldn't be competitive."

"Your sarcasm aside, it's a serious question. If you want to invest in another business, to diversify, I understand, but you know I'd be more comfortable with a smaller return on something closer to home."

Jake sipped coffee. "That's my pal Billy boy. Always ready to do something new and different as long as it's exactly the same." Then he smiled. "Just teasing, buddy." He always said that when I refused to go along with one of his plans, so I knew he was disappointed. My hand was resting on the table and he tapped the back of it. "You go home and forget about Ralph. I'll tell him that San Mateo Sparkle will stick to its core business in its hometown."

"Are you willing to let it go? If it's such a great opportunity—"

He shrugged. "Don't sweat it. If it makes you all jittery—" He stood up. "Your comfort is important to me."

"Since when?"

He turned toward the buffet. "Yesterday morning I saw something on the buffet called dragon fruit. That sounds intriguing. I need to explore."

I remembered it. "Weird looking stuff." I sighed. "But then you like taking risks," I said.

"Someone has to," he said.

"I wasn't talking about the damn fruit."

He smiled. "I know. And, as far as eating dragon fruit goes, given that, at a minimum a few million people have eaten it and survived, I don't see much risk there."

I watched him go to the buffet and fill a plate with all sorts of things I'd never seen before. Part of it was probably to taunt me. When he came back and sat down, I looked at him. "So, we agree we aren't investing in this company?"

His head bobbed as he chewed some kind of dumpling. "That's what I said."

"And you—"

"While I get a new passport, you go home and dream of van maintenance and cleaning teams and how we will adjust the cash flow to pay the payroll tax—all the things you enjoy worrying about."

His surrender, coming so easily, made me nervous. Jake had an affinity for Asia, and he'd been excited about this company—so excited that he'd made me come look at it.

"And you are going to go sightseeing while you wait for your new passport?"

Jake shook his head. "Don't trust me, Billy boy?"

"You've been known to go off on your own. I want you to remember that we have a business back home to run. And there are a couple of small outfits we were looking at acquiring—failing competitors. We were collecting data. If you want to expand—"

"I'm sure Betty will have incredible analytical summaries waiting for you when you get back," he said. "Feel free to take the appropriate actions. You and Betty have my blessing."

Betty is my twin sister. After college, she managed an office, quitting when she married Jake. That didn't work out well for a number of reasons, mostly because Betty is like me and Jake is… well, he is Jake.

For instance… being in our family meant spending every summer at a family gathering near Omaha. My parents had a place on Lake Carter, and Betty insisted he come along. It's likely our family's carefully planned vacations would have been enough to put the end to that relationship all by themselves.

The marriage lasted a couple of years. They never fought, just found life together a tiring tug of war. They had a son and Jake felt an obligation to stay married, but Betty, as conservative as she is, is also pragmatic. "It didn't work out," was her only comment.

After the divorce, they stayed on good terms. Meantime, our business grew like crazy, and when their son was a teen, Betty wanted to go back to work. Jake agreed, and we brought her into the company part time. I trained her to run the shop. Naturally, as it was a system I designed, and she is my sister, she fit in perfectly.

"You aren't comfortable going back home without me," he said, his mouth full of noodles.

"I worry about you getting involved in something here."

He waved a hand. "The world is filled with amazing things," he said. "I can't see turning a blind eye to them. And if they are a little risky, well, someone has to test the waters. But I won't obligate you in any way."

"I just worry."

"Of course you do. But think of it this way—if I hadn't started the cleaning business where would we be? Not here, for sure. And at the time, you thought it was silly."

The summary had enough truth to it to sting, although Jake's version was, as usual, a rather biased and narrow account. "If I hadn't insisted that we stop hiring illegals to do the work, we might be in jail."

Jake's eyes glistened. "Maybe. Or maybe we'd be even richer now." He sighed. "Besides, that wasn't you—it was a condition your old man put on loaning you the money."

I coughed. He was right. I wanted to make it seem I'd been noble, but it was my father's idea, and it was a practical matter, not idealism. He didn't want us getting shut down.

"It was the right thing to do. And as times and enforcement changed, it was a good move."

That earned me a grin. "Maybe so. What matters is that once you came on board, we built this business into something good—together, as a team, buddy."

"And why change things?"

"I've always thought my crazy ability to pick the risky ventures that could work and your ability to make them work would be unstoppable." As I let the obvious attempt to flatter me do exactly that, Jake looked around the room. "Look. I can go see live tigers and crocodiles at the Sri Racha Tiger Zoo," he said.

"What?"

"A zoo that specializes in tigers and crocodiles. I've never seen live crocs."

"I didn't know you wanted to."

"It's down on the Gulf of Thailand, to the south—a beach area. Ralph told me that it's only about 60 miles from here." I laughed, and he stared at me. "Tigers are funny?"

"No, but the image of you sightseeing at the zoo is."

He grinned his evil grin. "Depends on the sights there are to see. A croc might be worth the trip."

I remembered about his distaste for the family vacations. He'd told me, sarcastically: 'I need a vacation from the family vacation.' And now he'd go sightseeing?

"I can't see you sightseeing," I said. "You'd be bored."

He shrugged. "Well, I suppose I'll have to stay in Bangkok until I get the embassy drones started getting me a new passport. I can't expect they'll pop a new passport right out of the printer. It will take at least a couple of days for them to process things. I might not be a sightseer, but I can't just sit in a hotel room and watch television. I'll poke around. Ralph might have some ideas."

"I'm sure he will." Most likely none that I'd like. I looked at my watch. "Well, I need to get packed for the trip back."

"Give me a ring when you're ready and I'll ride out to the airport with you, make sure you get off safely," he said. He winked. "You can leave me any Baht you haven't spent. You won't have much use for Thai money in San Mateo."

This line of banter relaxed me. I knew damn well that seeing me off was just his way of ensuring I didn't go to the wrong airport (there were two in Bangkok) or do something equally stupid. It wasn't much comfort that he was right to worry. Outside of California, away from the family and the routine of running our cleaning business, I was out of my element as well as my comfort zone.

It might sound pathetic, but simply taking the trip had gotten me anxious. As the one running the day-to-day operations for our cleaning company, it was my job to worry that our cleaning crews weren't working to the standard I set for them. When I got back, I'd be phoning clients, making sure they were happy. I'd spend some time going over reports.

The thought of getting back to that made me relax. Once again I was struck with the contrast between my partner, my best friend, my brother-in-law and myself. I was looking forward to catching up on the basic things in life, and Jake, stuck in Bangkok without a passport, seemed happy as a clam.

Two roads diverged in a yellow wood,
And sorry I could not travel both
And be one traveler, long I stood
And looked down one as far as I could
To where it bent in the undergrowth;

Jake didn't make it back home for another week. During that time he called a couple of times to let us know that some Thai holiday had slowed the paperwork, and then to explain that although his new passport arrived, the airline screwed up his new reservation somehow. "Computers," said with great disdain, made up most of that discussion. "They can't get me on a flight for a couple of days."

I got the impression he didn't mind. "I'm sure you are heartbroken."

"I'll find some way to fill the time," he said.

Finally, on a Saturday, he sent me an email telling me it was all settled. "I've got an airport shuttle picking me up—it's late night arrival. I'll see you in the office Monday."

Monday morning, as I sat at my desk reviewing the spreadsheet I use to track the weekly schedule, my door opened and Jake walked. He was smiling and carrying two mugs of coffee. He held one out.

"Your espresso, sir. Two sugars, one milk."

I took the offered mug and watched a very relaxed Jake slip into the leather chair across from my desk.

"You must want something, stranger."

"Just an update. How's our wonderful world of cleaning?" he asked.

"Everything is on schedule," I told him.

He smiled. "Of course. Silly of me. You are in that chair and Betty is cracking the whip over the crews. All has to be right with world."

I laughed, but even after all the years working together, I still found it hard to know what my partner actually thought about what we did and our relationship. As with his marriage to Betty, the business had us, two quite different people, working hip to hip. I was confident he respected what I brought to the table, but what he thought of me as a person was something else.

"You look happy and relaxed," I said.

Jake sat back, holding his favorite coffee mug in both hands, looking at me over the top of it so I could see, "If you never try, you can't fail!" emblazoned on it in bright red letters.

Doreen had given him that mug at one of the office Christmas parties. He'd laughed when he opened it. I never understood why she picked that gift.

When I asked her what it meant, she'd just given me an odd look and said, "It's a joke."

"I don't get it."

She grinned. "You probably shouldn't even try to understand jokes."

Now that enigmatic slogan stared at me. "Was Ralph pissed when you told him the news?"

I saw surprise in his eyes. "The news?"

"That we decided not to invest."

"No. Why would he be?"

"Because he spent all that time with us and paid for the drinks…"

"Hell no. He knows it's just business. We were an option, nothing more."

He took a sip of coffee and glanced around my office. When he did that, I found myself wondering what he saw. I had things set up for efficiency. Flowcharts and a calendar (I still love paper calendars) were prominently displayed on the walls, along with a large photo of Doreen, the kids, and me at the folk's cabin on Lake Carter.

Jake's office was strange. The only things on the wall were a painting came with the office and a large poster with a photo of a tree-lined forest. Taken in fall, the trees had yellowing leaves. Robert Frost's famous poem, THE ROAD NOT TAKEN, was written over it. That's the poem about a man coming to a spot in the yellow woods where two roads diverged and having to pick one.

He'd had that poster for years. I'd never asked him what it meant to him. It didn't seem like Jake to regret much of anything. He always looked ahead.

"I'm glad you are back," I said now. "We took on both of those failing cleaning services we were looking at and hired several of their people. They are doing well."

His eyes glazed over for a moment, then he snapped his fingers. "Oh, right." I wondered if he knew what I was talking about. "Listen, I wanted to apologize," he said.

"For what?"

"Bangkok. Making you go. The whole thing."

"What whole thing?"

"Asia. Manufacturing." He laughed. "Ralph."

"I tried to tell you I didn't like the idea."

"But you know me… when I sense a good deal, I'm like a hunting dog on a scent. I can't let go of a good deal without a chase."

"A good deal?" I laughed. "Ralph runs a squalid sweat shop. The whole thing seems shady."

"No better or worse than most."

He made that sound like an endorsement. "Investing in it would be a gamble."

He pursed his lips. "Maybe. Some gambles pay off. Doreen said the books were good. Ralph has a track record of making money."

"That doesn't make it a good investment for us," I said firmly. I wanted this discussion to be over so I could put Thailand out of my head completely. I couldn't shake the images of the squalid nightlife.

Jake cupped his hands around his coffee mug, considering his words. "I thought I was being something you'd appreciate—prudent."

"Prudent?"

"I saw an opportunity. I thought we should go see the operation and make an assessment." He gave me a wistful smile. "I guess you made your decision before we left."

The dig struck home. "True, and I don't know what I could've said to make my position clearer. I never wanted anything to do with it."

He waved a hand. "Yes, you made it clear. The thing is… well, for several reasons the idea fired me up. I wasn't in a mood to hear any negativity."

That stunned me. "You didn't want to hear what I thought?"

"Not if it contradicted me." He pushed back in his chair. "You are my oldest friend, and over the years I've dragged you into more than one thing kicking and screaming. You were against developing the commercial end of our business, for instance. But I found us lucrative contracts. Once you saw the possibilities you were all for it."

"But that was—"

He held up a hand. "Different, I know. And I'm not offering an excuse. I'm trying to apologize and explain that sometimes I hear you saying no, and I hear you saying, 'make me do it.'" He smiled. "This time you meant it. I didn't treat your opinion with the dignity it deserved."

"It was a bad idea."

He looked at me. "Perhaps. At least by going over there you gave me the satisfaction of knowing you looked at the business opportunity closely and didn't just dismiss it out of hand."

"I suppose." For him, the outcome was what mattered.

"So, are we good?"

"We are fine," I said, not sure if that was true. "Maybe next time you will listen to what I say."

"I will."

Jake's answer came too quick for that. I've never trusted instant reassurances from anyone. They seem rehearsed and superficial. And now I wanted to change the topic. "Did you enjoy those extra days in Thailand?" I asked him.

A flicker of a smile crossed his face, and his eyes sparkled. "I did," he said. "A lot."

"The place put me off."

He grinned. "You didn't really see the country or meet any of the people. While I was there, I took some time to do that. They were amazing; I found I like the Thai people a lot."

"Really? I found them noisy and pushy."

My comment seemed to startle him, and for a moment, he sat still. "I found that they have a sense of dignity. Being among them made my time there peaceful."

I had to choke back a laugh. "Dignity?" I tried to relate that to my impressions of the country and failed.

"I'm not talking about the tourist touts," he said. "Cheap hustlers are the same, whether you encounter them in Naples or Bangkok. And the street sellers the worst of the lot."

"If you say so." Jake had been to both places. The brief stay in Thailand was my only experience outside of the US. "But dignity?"

He seemed to wake from a reverie then. "Just my impression," he said, standing. "I found being around them comforting, and I needed that." Before I could ask why he needed it, he was heading for the door. "If I am truly back, then I better get to work and follow up and get making cold calls. New business won't generate itself."

"Glad you're back," I said as he headed for the door.

I noticed that he didn't respond to that, but he did pause in the doorway where he turned back to give me a wistful look. "You know, Billy boy, we had a lovely tax-deductible trip to Thailand. There's something you can take off your bucket list."

Then he was gone, leaving me in a cloud of resentment. He knew damn well I hadn't had a lovely trip and that my bucket list, to the extent I had one, was limited to things like shooting par at the golf club or making enough money to be able to afford an infinity pool for the house. Visiting Thailand had been a chore, not some dream of mine. The allure of far-flung places was lost on me.

With the door closed behind him, I thought about that difference.

I was still stewing when I got home.

"I can tell Jake is back," Doreen laughed.

"He is."

"And he's frustrated you. Again."

"Yes. I don't understand him."

"How could you?" she asked. "You two live on different planets. Your idea of a perfect life is his worst nightmare, and his dream world would be a living hell for you."

"That's not true," I said far too quickly. "We both want the same things. Good people all generally want the same things."

"They do?" she asked. Her look suggested that the idea surprised her.

"I think so."

She shrugged. "Well, the thing is you need to accept the differences between you. They define the strength and weakness of your partnership and friendship," she said.

"I'm organized. He's visionary."

She smiled. "Something like that. You know, you and I are rather different kinds of people too… although the differences are less dramatic."

"We complement each other," I said. I knew what she meant. Her spontaneity and willingness, even eagerness, to try something new, often unsettled me. Still, I thought that by working out those differences, we strengthened our marriage.

I found her smile a tad enigmatic. "Maybe we do," she said.

"And I understand you… most of the time."

She kissed my cheek. "You think you do," she said. "That's enough."

I knew and loved Jake, and I think he felt the same. We did not have a single clue into what made the other tick, but in business we made a good team.

"Well, he's back in harness now, and life goes on."

"Okay," she said.

The next Saturday morning, after the kids had gone off with their friends, I settled myself at the dining table to go over the family finances. Yes, there are computer programs that do it for you, but I was old school. It kept thing manageable.

After a time, Doreen grabbed two bottles of cold beer from the refrigerator. I watched her pour one into a mug and smiled when she handed it to me. I took a grateful sip.

"I could do the books, you know," she said as she opened the other bottle. "I'm a trained professional."

I cringed as she took a long drink straight from the bottle. Betty and I grew up with the idea (the fact) instilled in us that bottles were dirty. "You don't know they cleaned them properly," Mom said. Given that firm conviction, anything less than pouring your drink, any drink, into a clean glass was unsanitary, and unsanitary was almost the worst thing in the world.

I'd never gotten used to the fact that Doreen loved her beer right from the bottle. It still surprised and, I'll admit, offended me. The way she'd look at me out of the corner of her eye as she drank gave me the impression that it delighted her that such a commonplace thing upset me.

I loved the woman, but she often irritated me. And yet, it was such a small thing. They usually are!

She nodded as she looked over my shoulder at the ledgers. "You do know that accounting, bookkeeping, projecting fiscal matters is what I do."

"I like to play with the numbers," I said. "I get satisfaction from seeing how we are doing."

She laughed. "Nonsense. It drives you crazy when numbers don't come out right."

"Of course it does. That only happens when I do something incorrectly."

She smiled. "I suppose. Still, I love tracking down the errors."

While she had the training and the experience and had been the company's accountant before we got married, I insisted on doing the accounts at home. That amused her too. She had several regular investors and small businesses that she worked for, keeping books, analyzing fiscal statements, and doing taxes.

"Doing our accounts would be no big deal for me, Bill. But you are a control freak who hates letting the books out of your hands."

I wondered if that was true. "I just like—"

"Being in control. That's why it was Jake's idea to bring Betty into the company, not yours. He asked her about it and she got excited. You just couldn't figure out how to tell your sister no."

"Not really."

"And that's why you don't want me coming back to work."

"I never said—"

"Right now, those numbers have you frowning. You aren't having fun, but you insist on torturing yourself."

"It's not torture."

"So why the scowl? Are we in trouble?" She sat down beside me.

I smiled. "No. Not trouble. Not at all."

Suddenly she laughed. "It's that damn infinity pool, isn't it?"

"It would be great for us and the kids."

Her grin cut through me. "Right. The kids want it. As if they are ever home for more than meals and a night's sleep these days."

I ignored the jibe. "The problem is, they are expensive. We'd have to buy it on credit and the payments would stretch us to the limit."

She shook her head. "That's only because your comfort zone is so narrow, darling."

Once again someone close to me was getting on me about wanting to be comfortable. "What's wrong with wanting to be comfortable. And anyway, this is a matter of being prudent."

"Being prudent, as you see it, defines the outer limits of your comfort zone."

When she said that sort of thing, and she said it often, I found it pointless to ask for an explanation. Not that she would refuse to tell me what she meant. She would try, but her rationale always escaped me.

"We'd be overextended."

She tipped her head. "You make that sound like a bad thing."

"You are just being nasty now."

"Actually, I'm serious. What would happen if you acted imprudently—just once?"

I shuddered. "That wouldn't be sensible. It would be irrational."

"And there's no doubt that you are sensible."

"I hear a 'but' in that."

She sipped her beer. "Have you ever considered that we are where we are financially because we act sensibly and prudent. And Jake, insensible as he is, gets more of what he wants."

That held enough truth to hurt. "He takes risks."

"You get jealous over that fancy house in Half Moon Bay that he and Betty bought, his fancy car, and the expensive vacations he takes."

It struck me, not for the first time, that Doreen admired Jake's sense of adventure. So where did that leave me in her view? Somewhat parochial, I imagined. Not that it upset her. On the contrary, one of the things about her that amazed me was how she acted as if everything that went on was a play being staged for her amusement.

Bringing up the house seemed like a cheap shot. Doreen and I owned our nice house in Hollister. It was a nice area, but nothing flashy. (And nothing like the house Jake had bought and signed over to Betty during the divorce).

"I still don't know how Jake could afford that place," I said.

Doreen surprised me by laughing. "Don't you guys talk? Don't you talk to your sister?"

"What do you mean?"

"Your sister said that when they found it, the place was in foreclosure. Jake made a cash offer. He sold some investment, and that was it."

"Cash?" It was hard to imagine having my hands on that kind of money. "Betty and I don't talk about money," I said. "You must've asked."

"Of course, I did. Tight-lipped Betty never would have told me, otherwise. I know that family trait too."

That she could pry the information loose from Betty came as no surprise. Doreen could make people open up. It never occurred to me to ask such questions. "I have trouble believing he had that much in investments."

She held up her empty bottle. "Wait!" Then she went in the kitchen, coming back with two more, pouring mine into my glass before provocatively putting her own, open, dirty, on the table. "You shouldn't have to believe it. Jake never makes a secret of his investments. You are always mentioning some scheme or another he thinks you should put money into. The problem is that you don't really trust him."

That shocked me. "Of course, I trust him. He's my partner."

She patted my hand. "I'm not saying you don't think he's honest."

"What else could you mean?"

"His judgment. You don't trust his judgment."

"Sure, I do."

She shook her head. "Really. It doesn't seem so."

"Why would you even say that? After all these years—"

Her eyebrow lifted. "Well, I figure that if you trusted him, you'd have gone in on some of his investments. But you don't."

I shook my head, but it didn't make things clearer. "What are you saying?"

"That when he comes up with investment ideas, you dismiss them."

"If one seemed right…"

That had her laughing again. "In all these years, not one, besides the cleaning company, has ever seemed right to you, and never will. And the only reason you are in the cleaning business is because your father invested his money to get you a partnership."

"Because I asked him to. Jake wanted to expand."

"And you've never trusted his judgment enough to put your own money into anything."

As I pondered that, trying to decide if it was true, she pursed her lips.

"Remember the time he came over all excited and tried to get you to buy into that bakery?"

I let out a breath. "A risky proposition. The guy wanted to sell because the big chains were killing his business. There's no way to compete with those guys."

She sighed and smiled. "You remember it that way."

"How do you remember it?"

"The business was in trouble because of piss poor management. If you recall, Jake had me go over the books before he came to you. I saw no problems with their finances, and I told you that. I even told you then that Jake's idea of spinning the business into a boutique bakery for upscale customers—catering, special events, things like that, sounded good."

"That's a real challenge."

"Not for a debt-free business with low overhead. If the owner had wanted to do the work, he could've made it profitable himself."

It didn't pay to disagree with Doreen's fiscal analysis, so I changed tactics. "You need to remember that money was tight for us back then."

"You think it wasn't' tight for Jake? When you didn't go in on it, he had to borrow everything he could to raise the money. Last year he sold the business and made a bundle."

I hadn't known that. "What's your point? Jake got lucky."

Doreen stared at me. "Seriously? Lucky? You think luck is why his investments almost always make money?"

I sipped my beer. It tasted bitter, even from a clean glass. "When you take enormous risks, luck is always a factor. I'm not comfortable doing that."

She sighed again. "That's fine. No one expects you to be anyone other than who you are. I'm just saying you are a control freak. As long as you accept that it isn't a problem. But it means you can't begrudge him his money."

"I'm just not a gambler. I need to know my investments are safe. That way I can sleep nights."

It hurt that she laughed at that. "I hope you know that 'safe investment' is a contradiction in terms, right? An investment is a gamble. The riskier gambles earn the most return precisely because of the risk. But you'd rather stay in your comfort zone without the pool than take a risk."

"Better be safe than sorry," I said.

"I know that's your motto, Bill."

It was only later that I found myself wondering if she'd meant that as a compliment. I tried to convince myself that was how she'd meant it.

After the talk we'd had, Jake never brought up Thailand again. In fact, it seemed that he was avoiding me. That made me wonder if he was sulking. But that was foolish. Jake wasn't the kind to sulk. He'd laugh at what he saw as my foolishness and move on.

As we got our newly acquired crews up to speed, I expected Jake to come in with some new business, but that didn't seem to be happening. Under normal circumstances, he'd swoop into a staff meeting and cheerfully ask how many new clients we could handle. Betty noticed too and made some remark about him being off his game.

When I heard him snap at the receptionist over a minor matter, that made me really start to worry. Mattie was a cute young woman and Jake loved teasing her, being charming and flirting, even when she upset him. She could be careless at times but reprimanding her always fell to me.

His attention was somewhere else. The man who rushed into the office, eager to make cold calls, to chat up big clients, hadn't come back from Asia. He still worked the phone, but the calls I overheard lacked even a little enthusiasm. He had no fire.

When I asked him if everything was okay, he just brushed me off. It went against the grain to probe. Our family had a saying: It's rude to intrude.

But I noticed him taking time off, coming in late, sometimes staying out the entire day.

"I assume he's got a new transitory girlfriend," Betty said. He'd dated frequently since their divorce, but never gotten serious about anyone.

That day I as I stared out my window (daydreaming) into the courtyard, Jake sat on the bench talking on his phone. I could see the frustration on his face. That got my curiosity in high gear, I can tell you. Jake never minded making his calls in front of people.

That night, I shared my concerns with Doreen. "It's like he is still partly there," I told her.

"Where?"

"Bangkok. Asia." I gave her a hopeless look. "Somewhere else. His attention certainly isn't here, not focused on the business. And Jake has always been someone who lives in the moment."

She rubbed her chin. "That doesn't sound like him."

"And I think it's my fault."

"Bullshit," she said. "What could you do that would cause him to change like that?"

I struggled to figure out how to explain. "It's just a theory, but I get the distinct impression that the trip to Asia meant more to him than I understood."

"Like he wanted a major change?"

"Maybe. Or a sign. It could be symbolic. Whatever it was, my unwillingness to take that gamble, to do business in Bangkok disappointed him." I looked at Doreen. "It's as if I shit on a dream that was precious to him and in the process, showed him my true, conservative nature."

"He's always known who you are. If that surprised him even a little, he's dumber than I think."

"But not the depth of my conservative nature. On that trip… it's never been so clear that we look through opposite ends of the microscope. Everything excited him; everything I saw repelled me. I'm thinking he took that personally. It's like I rejected him."

She stared out the window. "A wounded pride, or unhappiness with you might explain him withdrawing and being out of sorts, but it not why he's making secretive phone calls."

"I didn't mean I could explain everything."

"No."

"Another thing… he has barely talked about the days he spent alone in Asia. When I've chickened out on some adventure of his, he's always loved to tease me about what I missed. The time he went skiing in Aspen he came back with hundreds of stories. I expected to hear about the great meals he ate, the fun he had. But he's been cryptic—hardly said a thing."

She put her hands on her hips. This was her stern thinker pose. "Maybe whatever is wrong has nothing at all to do with you or the trip? What if it isn't about you?"

"It is about me if it goes on. It could interfere with business.

"Why do you say that?"

"He snaps at Mattie, for one thing. That's not good. And even though he's still talking to the clients, it isn't the same. He's going through the motions. His heart isn't in it."

"Maybe you are misjudging things."

I doubted that. "The other day, a client called and told him she needed to reschedule several cleaning jobs. But I didn't hear about until she called me to find out what the new schedule was. I stalled her, told her we were trying to work it out. I had to pretend it was a mixup." I pushed my chair back.

"Did you ask him about it?"

"Yes, and he seemed pissed at me for bringing it up. He said not to worry, and she'd get over it, whatever that means."

I watched her consider that. Her look showed concern. "Something is wrong."

"Another thing. You know how spartan hc keeps his office. Now he's covered the walls with travel posters of tropical destinations. I've seen him staring at them wistfully."

She raised a finger. "A subtle hint?" she asked, smiling. "If he wants to go back to see more of Asia isn't necessarily a bad thing."

"That's what I thought. Maybe he needs to go back and get Asia out of his system. I walked in and stared at the posters. 'Planning another trip?' I asked. All he said was, 'life is short.'"

"You need to ask him right out. Or bring him here and I'll ask him."

"He'll tell me if something big is wrong."

"Will he? Fuck that. Jake is your friend. If he isn't acting like one, then you need to point that out. Get in his face and let him know that you are concerned about him and are there for him. Surely you can do that, at least."

"I tried."

She smirked. "Really."

"I said he wasn't acting like himself."

"That isn't exactly asking."

"He said it was probably a good thing. Then he smiled and went in the courtyard to make another phone call. He's shutting me out."

She sighed and shook her head. "Don't let him. You need to step up. Ask the damn question."

"You said that."

She held her hands open. "What else can I say?"

My wife can be damn irritating. It's always worst when she is right.

The next morning, I arrived and found his office door wide open. I poked my head in to see him sitting at his desk, smiling at me over his coffee. I hesitated. Despite the smile, despite the hearty good morning he'd thrown at me, I was taken with how frail he looked. I hadn't noticed before.

I took a seat across from him and his eyebrows raised. "Is this the Spanish Inquisition?"

It was his favorite Monty Python routine.

"Not if you tell me what I want to know." That was my attempt to keep it light hearted.

He leaned forward. "I know nothing at all. But that's a secret. Don't even tell me."

I think Jake could deflect an inquisition. I jumped right in. "What's going on with you, Jake?" I asked.

"What do you mean?"

"For one thing, you look like shit."

He grinned and hoisted his mug. "Not fair. I'm only on my first cup of coffee. Life doesn't start until after that. I have come to the conclusion that evolution began with the discovery of coffee. I've let the Nobel committee know of my findings and expect to hear from them any day."

"Well, that's certainly a major step forward for science, but if I ask something personal, will you answer?"

He sat his mug down and looked at me. "Ask me anything, old buddy," he said. Given the circumstances, his sincerity embarrassed me.

"Are you upset with me?"

That seemed to shock him. "With you? No. Why would you ask that?"

I ticked off the reasons on my fingers. "Because you don't answer my questions, because you look like shit even after many cups of coffee, although you keep saying you are fine, and because you sneak into the courtyard to make phone calls."

"Is that all?" he said. Then he broke out laughing. "I guess that does sound fishy as hell."

"I feel you are keeping me in the dark—that you have secrets you are keeping from me."

"If I tell you, the NSA says I'll have to kill you."

"I'm serious."

He sighed. "Okay. Serious it is. I do have secrets from you, Billy boy. Too many. Do you really want to know what they are?"

"Yes. I want to help, if I can."

"Well, you can't and don't want to help with the first one. Secret number one: I invested in Ralph's manufacturing operation."

"You said you wouldn't."

He shook his head. "No. I said we wouldn't. I used my own money and left you out of it—at your insistence."

"And you lost it?" That would explain the way he looked.

He grinned. "Negative. It's already turning a profit." He laughed, and I wondered if it was at my expense.

"That was fast."

"I told you that Ralph had everything lined up. I handed over the money before I left, and by the end of the week he was cranking out toys. With US government putting pressure on manufacturers to get out of China, he's had to turn customers down. He wants me back in Thailand to look at plans for the next level of expansion."

"Next level?"

"We are looking at building a new plant. Well... buying and refitting one near Chang Mai. That leads me to secret number two: I'm heading back to Thailand. Ralph wants me to see the new place."

The knot in my stomach that had begun showing up when I talked business with Jake grew painful. "Does that mean that all this, the cleaning business, isn't important any longer?" Or me, I thought.

He grinned. "Not at all. But I'm looking at winding down my role. You guys are kicking ass with this business. Skipping the humble bullshit, I was vital in getting it here, but you and Betty are the management gurus."

"You are the face of the business."

He held up a hand. "I suggest that we bring Doreen back into the fold."

"What?"

"That woman is bored, and we both know she is more than capable of taking over the books from the outside firm and doing my job as well. Probably better than I can. And I bet she'd jump at it."

My heart sank. He was right. "What about you? Will you stay in Asia?"

He paused, wincing briefly. "No. I have to figure it out."

My heart skipped a beat. Jake was cutting himself loose from the world that I had assumed would go on forever as it was. He wanted out. "You want to quit?"

"Something besides business in Asia needs my attention," he said.

"What?"

He turned his coffee cup. "Pain management." Silence filled the room. "I'm suffering chronic pain. My doctor put me on meds for pain about a year ago. They helped at first, but it was getting worse and the meds made me feel like shit. Part of the reason I wanted to go to Thailand was to visit a clinic there. The doc said they have access to techniques that aren't approved here... yet."

"You didn't lose your passport."

"No. But I couldn't talk you into staying, and I didn't think you'd like me staying behind."

"Did they help you?"

"Not as much as I would've liked. They have other, longer therapies that could do something. I went back on the meds when I came back, but they make me irritable and I can't focus. I'm assured that continuing to take the drugs will make the side effects get worse. I've decided to go back and try a two-week program. So, you see, bringing in Doreen to take over for me is our best option."

I tried to picture the business, my life, without Jake around all the time. It was like watching a friend go off to explore the unknown. I had no desire to tag along, yet somehow felt like I was being left in the dust.

"I don't understand. Doreen can fill in for you, but why not take some treatments and then come back to work?"

He shrugged. "It isn't clear that any treatments will do the trick, and I'm tired of pretending I'm not in pain—not that I've done that well lately."

I couldn't think of a reply, an alternative that I could insist he try. "I'm sorry. You go get well."

"I've got a business lead for you and Doreen to follow up on," he said as cheerfully as if we'd been discussing him going on vacation.

"What is the new job? Cleaning up after space launches?" I asked, my voice dripping with a ton of nasty that I hadn't realized was lurking there.

"Nothing so profitable," he laughed. "I had lunch with a realtor, following up on my idea. She is

expanding her business... renting out office spaces."
He wrote down a name and phone number and
pushed it across the desk. "Give that to Doreen. I
talked to this woman briefly and I think she could
give us a hell of a lot of business. If I won't be here,
it's better if you two make the pitch."

Taking it, feeling the finality of the moment,
made me numb.

"While I'm in Thailand, maybe Doreen should
give Space-X a shout."

"Space-X?"

"Follow up on your idea about cleaning up after
launches. That has to make a hell of a mess. It could
be a new specialty. Way to think out of the box,
partner."

Jake was right about Doreen being up for the
challenge. "I only hate that the reason I'm doing this
is that Jake is suffering," she said.

We all felt that way.

She arranged a meeting with Jake's contact, and after a brief conversation, Jake's optimism infected her. "This will be big for us," she said.

"What is it?" I asked.

"Offices," she said. "But this woman is moving fast. She will be a serious player.

When she seated us in her office, it only took a moment to see that Doreen had sized up the realtor perfectly. Her office was as spartan as Jake's used to be, and she was a no-nonsense businesswoman in a hurry.

"I'm glad you called me," she said. "I think we can do business."

"Business is good, then?" I asked.

"It's crazy good. I've had a couple of office buildings for a time, but with the failure of some of the tech companies, I'm expanding. Those startups build lovely industrial parks. Right now, if I act fast, I can get them in foreclosure." She grinned. "They build them, I buy them and rent them out."

"And there is demand?" Doreen asked.

She threw her head back, laughing. "Demand? I've got people screaming for decent, well-managed office space. I'll charge a premium and that's where you come in. My clients want to move into spotless offices and not have to think about maintenance." She shook her head in dismay. "Unfortunately, some people are pigs, and these spaces need serious cleaning before I can lease them, and when that's done, I need to be able to guarantee routine cleaning as part of the deal."

Doreen nodded. "Of course. That's what we do."

"I'll want a contract that includes light cleaning of the entire complexes three nights a week—empty the trash, vacuum the rugs, clean windows, clean and restock bathrooms—"

"Standard stuff."

"I want a major cleaning, including carpets, once a quarter." She shuffled through some papers. "I've got bids from a couple of companies for the grounds, but if you know anyone…"

"We have a company that does that well," Doreen said confidently. "I'll send you a bid for the entire package." My pulse was racing. I forced myself to be quiet even though my brain was screaming out that doing all this meant adding teams, buying new equipment… and Doreen was simply taking the order as if it was just another house to clean. "My bid will be based on a firm commitment—a one-year contract to start."

The woman nodded and handed Doreen a folder. "This describes the facilities and gives you the square footage. I want an estimate for doing them all and a promise from you that you will expand to accommodate me if I add more. I'm looking at a service bay out at the airport."

Doreen looked at the pages and handed them to me. "I'll need to do a walk-through," Doreen said. "It all looks different when you are there."

The woman nodded. "My secretary has the keys and can meet you whenever you want to check them out."

A quick glance told me this was a massive amount of work. "We will need to add people as well as some more trucks and equipment. We should talk to Jake."

Doreen shook her head. "Are the people available?"

I ran the teams through my head. "If we promote some workers into team leaders and add the new ones into existing teams they can train on site. So yes. I'm more worried about going into debt for the trucks."

"We won't," Doreen said. She looked at the realtor. "I'll get you a bid by tomorrow morning, if that's okay."

"If we come to an agreement, I'd set up a monthly autopay." Then she paused. "Can you accept payment in Bitcoin?"

"We prefer cash," I said.

Doreen put a hand on my arm. "Bill runs our operations. He has an ingrained fear of new financial, like crypto, but I run finance. I'm restructuring things and, while we don't take Bitcoin at the moment, I'd be delighted to set up a wallet. I'll send you the QR code along with our estimate."

For the first time, the realtor smiled. "That's so perfect. I do like doing business with people who enjoy making things happen."

Making things happen—that described Doreen, I thought. And Jake too... the old Jake. For now, Doreen was a wonderful new Jake. She might even be more Jake than Jake. And, like Jake, there seemed to be things she wasn't telling me.

The next weeks were filled with all that goes with ramping up business. It was crazy, and I was glad when Betty came in full time. Working together, we made it happen.

"Jake's back," Betty told me.

"He didn't call. How is he?"

"I don't exactly know, even though he's staying with me. He asked me to get everyone together this weekend. He's being dramatic and wants to tell everyone his news all at once."

Betty doesn't think much of people who are being dramatic.

"And you don't have a clue?" I asked.

"I don't speculate." Her schoolteacher grimace put me in my place. "Just get over to my house Saturday afternoon. I'll make a huge vat of spaghetti and we will send the kids off to eat in the television room."

"Why?"

"Because the television room has vinyl floors and wiping up the inevitable spilled sauce isn't a big deal?"

"I mean, why have the kids eat separately?"

Betty sneered. "Because I'm sure Jake feels the need to be grown-up dramatic over wine or something stronger and they don't really know what's going on. He's going to rent some new movie that Doreen said they are clamoring to see."

With the turmoil at work I found myself looking forward to a relaxing get together and hearing how the new therapy had gone. Seeing him made my stomach knot up. He'd lost even more weight and his pale skin told me he hadn't gotten any beach time.

"How are you?" I asked as we settled into chairs on the patio.

"First—" Jake held up a bottle of a whisky that I'd only heard about. It was absurdly expensive. I couldn't help but think of the cost of each glass as he poured out healthy drinks, neat. "Now, I know I owe you all, each of you, an explanation. You deserve to know what is going on. But first a toast. *L'chaim*— to life"

Not one of us had a snappy reply to that. I sipped my drink, and the others did the same. Jake drank, then took a deep breath.

"The trip I took to Thailand wasn't successful."

"Their pain therapies didn't work?" I asked.

"That's no surprise," Betty said. "If they worked, then doctor's here—"

"When I came back, I didn't come straight here. I made a side trip up to the Mayo clinic in Phoenix. That wasn't productive either, except in confirming the diagnosis."

"I thought it was chronic pain."

He paused to taste his drink again. "Damn that's fine stuff. Anyway, the thing is I've been lying. Now I have to come clean. I don't have a chronic condition."

"That's a relief," I said.

"Is it?" He sighed. "Sorry, I'm being flip. It isn't a relief. You see chronic means 'continuing or occurring again and again for a long time.' I looked it up. That makes this a rare situation because the doctors and the dictionary agree on something."

"So your pain isn't chronic?"

"No. You see, although it does continue and reoccurs, it won't persist for the long time that makes it chronic."

"I told you he wanted to be dramatic," Betty said.

The look in Jake's eyes told me the story didn't have a happy ending. "What do you mean? Tell us the rest."

He cocked his head. "You see, I'm dying."

"That's absurd," Betty said. "You are only in your fifties—a young man."

"A young man dying of colon cancer," he said calmly.

"What exactly did the doctors say?" Betty demanded.

"A lot of shit," he said. "Most of it contradictory or doesn't make sense. But it all comes down to the fact that I have much less than a year to live."

"We need a second opinion," Betty said. "Doctors make mistakes."

He shook his head slowly. "I've already been to three doctors and more specialists. They all speak the same party line."

"Can't they operate?" I asked.

Jake leaned back and laughed as if I'd told a grand joke. "Of course they can operate. They love to operate. They want to remove infected tissue from my kidneys."

"I thought you had colon cancer," I said.

"The fun fact about colon cancer is that it spreads to other organs. They can cut out the bad bits, but it won't cure me." He sighed. "And I tried their poisons the last time."

"You had it before?"

He nodded. "Last year. They did some magic at a clinic here—dosed me up as an outpatient. I felt like shit, but it seemed to work. I went into remission. But it came back in spades. The clinic in Thailand has access to drugs that US doctors aren't allowed yet. That's what this last trip was about."

"And it didn't help?"

"After a consultation and some tests, they said my cancer is too advanced. Their treatment would kill me. Ironically, as I told you I was going for pain therapy, all they gave me was pain pills."

Betty swallowed. "What do our doctors recommend?"

"That I prepare to die. They think I should accept the inevitability of going into a hospice and dying pumped up with a laundry list of drugs and radiation treatments. I think they are full of shit, personally."

"As usual," Betty said, "you know more than the doctors."

"In this case, they are the ones saying they don't know anything. At least I know what I want."

"And what the hell would that be?" Betty asked. I could hear anger, shock, fear churning in her voice.

"I've talked to a hospital in Bangkok. They are developing an experimental treatment that seems to have a real cure rate."

"Real?" I asked. "What does that mean?"

"Greater than zero." He grinned. "That's a damn sight better than the odds I'm offered here."

Betty gave him a look of disbelief. "You want to go to some filthy hospital Asia and let those people treat you?"

Jake put a hand on hers. "Betty, I've seen it. It is modern and clean and the only place in the world that offers this treatment." He handed us brochures. "I had these printed from their website."

As we looked over the material, I could feel Betty's anger building. "This is just New Age garbage. It's coffee enemas and such."

"The program I'm looking at involves extensive vitamin therapy, specialized diets, and work in a hyperbaric chamber."

Betty sneered. "That's not medicine."

Jake sighed. "No, it isn't. But the doctors here tell me there is no medicine that will work for me, Betty. All they can do is prolong my life—make it take longer for me to die. This Thai hospital offers me some hope and ensures my dignity." Jake pointed to a line at the bottom of her copy of the brochure. "This is the part I like."

Betty squinted to read it. We'd all been after her to get glasses, but she was as stubborn as, well, as everyone in our family. Holding the brochure close, she read the statement: "We promise to do our best to cure you. Failing that, we ensure you a death with dignity." When she finished, she put the brochure down and looked up at him. "Would you like to tell me what in the world you like about that?"

Jake looked excited. "It's something I've thought about a lot. I think it is a beautiful phrase: Death with Dignity."

"A beautiful phrase? You want to leave us and run halfway around the world for a phrase?"

"No. For dignity. I can't stand the thought of letting doctors fill my body with chemicals that turn me into little more than a sick vegetable and stick tubes in me to keep me alive well past my shelf life."

"Don't joke about it! This isn't funny," Betty said.

"No it isn't," Jake said. "None of it is funny." He touched her hand again. "I'm looking at this the same way I've always approached my investments. I do my research and pretty often turn out to be right."

"That's true," I said without thinking.

Betty glared at me. "We are talking about your life, not an investment."

"Betty, I am dying. The chances of this cure working are slim but, if their treatment fails, I will avoid dying in a hospice, surrounded by the smell of disinfectant and forced to take medicine by the clock. I can't stand the thought of such an undignified way."

Doreen sighed. She was still reading the brochure. "They say they help you die… in comfort."

Betty looked confused. "Comfort. That's why the doctors give out pain pills. When I had my gall bladder surgery—remember how they kept me all doped up. It was glorious."

"I'm not afraid of the pain, Betty. I'm afraid of not feeling it. Living dead to the world isn't living, and it isn't dignified."

"So, you are ready to give up!"

"Just the opposite. I intend to try a Hail Mary play in a Buddhist country and see how that works for me."

"It isn't funny!" She was almost screaming now.

"Betty, I'm going to do this. I'm not asking permission. I just needed you all to know what was going on. I've made the arrangements."

Just as with his investments, Jake had done his research and made up his mind. We could go along or disapprove, but that wouldn't change a thing. What any of us thought was irrelevant.

Betty frowned at me when I got to their house. That was becoming her default expression. "He's in the bedroom packing," she said.

I found him staring at a nearly empty suitcase. "Traveling light?"

He gave me a strange smile. "I find myself wondering just how much a dying man needs to lug around the world with him."

"Enough to have clean clothes for the trip home after he gets out of the clinic, at least."

He gave me a sharp look. "Are you a believer now?"

I laughed. "No, but I think if you intend to try a Hail Mary, you need to take the attitude that it will work. That's what you told me about all the gambles you took."

He nodded. "Who would have known you were even listening when I said that? Okay, then I should pack for a round trip."

"Sure. Even if their treatment doesn't work, your doctors said you'll have as much as a year, and maybe more."

I saw him tense. "Oh yes, but that year is predicated on letting them stick me with needles, on lying in a bed with tubes feeding me for most of that time. That isn't living."

"It is living. None of us want to lose you."

"You have already," he said. "Orson Welles said: 'We're born alone, we live alone, we die alone. Only through our love and friendship can we create the illusion for the moment that we're not alone.' I have no patience with illusions. Your sister is going to have to go on without me and delaying dealing with that won't help her or me. This disease is like experiencing a car wreck in slow motion. It's already happened, but you have to live through it."

"Betty found an article that says the Mayo Clinic is trying a new procedure that extends life for patients with your symptoms."

"I don't want the life of my symptoms extended," He said. "Sorry. Bad joke. She showed me the article.

The treatment sounds dreadful." He tossed a pair of swim trunks in the bag. They were decorated with palm trees.

"I haven't seen those before," I said.

He grinned. "Not exactly the thing for Carter Lake, are they? In Thailand, I won't be in the hospital all the time. I've decided to spend free time on the beach. Maybe I can die with a decent tan."

"I see the cancer hasn't spread to your sense of humor gland. But I don't see those trunks doing much to add to your dignity."

He cocked his head. "Well, your sense of humor seems to have improved."

He was right. Black humor had always offended me, and here I was joking about cancer. "I'm in shock. Trying to lighten the mood, I guess."

"Aren't we all?"

"The thing is, I can't come back to this, Billy boy."

"To what?"

"To some incarceration in a hospital. Betty doesn't get it, but I'm at a crossroads."

"That makes no sense."

He sat on the bed. "Look. You know me as well as anyone. Better than Betty. If you had to say what I lived for—being totally honest—what would you say that is?"

"Adventure. Risk."

He nodded. "I've sought thrills. I couldn't have run a business they way you do. The routine would kill me. And there is a dynamic there. How do you think I'd do confined to bed in a drug-induced stupor?"

"Not so good."

"Now, I could run around the world chasing cures. If this one doesn't work, hell, there are lots of them out there, and I can spend my money running from one to the next."

"No. You couldn't."

He smiled. "Exactly. That takes two options off the list. What does that leave?"

"Dying without doctors or cures."

"Right."

"Giving up? That's not your style."

"No. Not giving up. That's a sucker game. I'm talking about embracing the best option."

"Death with dignity?"

I saw my answer pleased him. "Here we are... back to that again. I can give this cure a try, but if it fails—"

"Come back and let us take care of you."

He sighed. "I can't do that, Billy boy."

For once, he made that dreadful nickname sound truly affectionate. "Then?"

"I don't want to tell Betty, but I won't be back. I have to follow my bliss."

"Does that mean you intend to buy Thailand?"

Jake shot me a look, then burst out laughing. "I hadn't thought of that. Good one."

"Then what?"

"You know that from the time I was little, I wanted to be rich."

"And you are."

He sighed. "Did I ever talk about my fallback plan?"

That made me laugh. "I've never considered you needed one. It's hard to imagine you not plunging ahead."

"Well, it's not so much a fallback plan as my alternative goal—the life I'd choose to live, I dreamed of, if my early plans didn't work out. See, I always saw myself as either getting rich or hiding in some idyllic place."

"Thailand, for example."

"He nodded. But without all this. With no investments to think about, no business to run."

"And doing what?"

"Living in the moment."

"The anti-Jake."

That amused him. "To a degree. The anti-Jake in his beautiful, alternative universe." He held up the swim trunks and looked at them as if there was a message in the fabric. "There's something to be said for living each moment as if it is our last. A lot to be said for it. And when I had that dream of peace instead of prosperity, it never occurred to me that I might be spending my money to go to an idyllic place because my last moments were coming at me so fast." He dropped the trunks in the suitcase again. "There's an irony in that."

"And this other life you dreamed of… that's what the poster is about, isn't it?"

He grinned. "You are full of insight and surprise today."

"Two roads and now you wonder about the one you didn't take. That's the theme, right?"

He nodded.

> *Two roads diverged in a wood, and I—*
> *I took the one less traveled by,*
> *And that has made all the difference.*

He twisted to smile at me. "Unlike Frost, when I reached that fork, I took the one more traveled by. I wanted money and success. Now, when I'm forced to confront my life, I wonder what it would have been like if I'd taken the other."

"And where does that road lead that you'd want to go? You love adventure."

"Adventures lie along both paths, I'm sure."

"Are you telling me that after all this time you regret your choice?"

He smiled. "Not at all. It's just that the other represents the great what-if. What if I'd gone that way?"

"We wouldn't have started the business; you wouldn't have married Betty."

"All true. My life would have been different. What I think about, what I wonder is if by taking that path my adventures would have had me chasing peace and dignity instead of money."

"You've enjoyed your money."

"I enjoyed making it and spending it up to a point. But it lost its luster quickly. In the beginning, I wanted Xanadu."

"What?"

"Another poem."

> *"In Xanadu did Kublai Khan*
> *A stately pleasure-dome decree:*
> *Where Alph, the sacred river, ran*
> *Through caverns measureless to man*
> *Down to a sunless sea.*

Suddenly I had an idea. "You should take Betty with you."

"What?" He gave me an astonished look. "What for?"

"She still cares. She'd be there to help you, take care of you."

He stroked his chin. "And Betty would agree, because she'd see it as her duty. But can you imagine Betty sitting in a Bangkok hotel room all day while I get treatment? I can't. First of all, she doesn't believe in what I'm doing. She thinks that I'm throwing money away on quacks. More to the point, without ever seeing the place, she hates the idea of Asia. She'd be miserable there."

I couldn't argue that point. "Then I could go."

That earned a laugh. "You don't like Asia much more than she does. Why should my miserable ending be an excuse to make you suffer any more than her? I'd feel guilty about putting you through that."

"But you'll be all alone."

He trembled slightly. "We die alone, like Welles said. I intend to deal with it"

I wanted to offer sage advice, a bit of wisdom, but none came to mind and trying to force some nugget to the surface made me dizzy. Truthfully, I fancied myself a pragmatic person, and what Jake said made perfect sense. Yet, part of me rebelled against his decision.

"Then this is it? We won't see you again?"

He held his hands out. "Unless the hospital comes up with some high-quality magic none of us can even imagine, I suspect it will be our last chat, Billy boy."

He took my hand. The frailness of his grip shocked me, and I found myself pulling him into a hug.

Jake patted my back. "You are a good friend and a great partner. Betty is lucky to have you for a brother."

I didn't trust myself to say another word. He took up his bag and left. I never saw him again.

After Jake flew out of SFO, Doreen and I took care of some paperwork for his treatment. Our company self-insured medical care for the owners of the company, and I had to authorize payments to the Thai hospital. At their instructions, I had Jake's doctors send his medical files to them. I took a strange comfort in doing something, however superficial.

The next morning, we had Betty come over to the house for breakfast. While we were eating, she got a call from Jake. I put it on speakerphone. "It was a great flight," he said, sounding enthusiastic.

"Where are you?" I asked.

"I just checked in to my hotel. Tomorrow I'm going to see Ralph."

"What about your treatment?" Betty asked.

"That is scheduled to start in a couple of days. This evening I'm meeting Ralph. We will take care of some business. Remember that once I'm admitted I'll be out of touch for a time."

"If you are going to be out of touch, how will we know how you are doing?" Betty demanded.

"I don't know, exactly," he said. "All I can ask is that you try not to worry. If the doctors have news, if there are promising signs, I'll call."

Betty wasn't appeased. "What if it goes badly?"

There was a long silence. Finally, Jake spoke softly. "Betty, bad news is the most likely outcome. If you aren't hearing from me, that will be because there is no good news, and I don't want to give you any bad news. But don't worry—everything is taken care of."

"What is taken care of?"

"The business—"

"Do you mean money? That isn't what I was worrying about, fool."

"I'm taking care of everything that it is within my power to take care of, Betty. I might take risks, but I try not to leave things to chance." He let out a sigh. "I don't seem to be in control of much at the moment. I thought I knew myself, but I'm learning a great deal I didn't know."

"Damn it, Jake," she said, "you know yourself better than anyone I've ever known."

"Remember when I went to that weekend Buddhist retreat a few years ago."

Betty's lip curled. "Of course. While we were in Omaha."

"They taught that everything you think you know is illusion."

I laughed. "Good thing you aren't a Buddhist."

That made him laugh. "I'll call as soon as there is any good news."

We never heard from him again.

Betty and I got busy ramping up the business to meet our demanding new client's needs. Doreen took over the financials. Combining our efforts, we managed to whip everything into shape.

One day, Betty came in all worked up. "Enough is enough," she said. "It's time to do something."

"Do something?"

"About Jake," she said. "It's been a month since he called to say he was starting treatment. We should have heard something since then, good or bad."

"That long? Damn." I couldn't believe it. "I guess I should make some calls."

Betty snorted. "I did that much. The hotel said he checked out. The hospital wouldn't give me information at all. I called the US embassy in Bangkok. Three times. Officially, they weren't the least bit helpful," she said.

"And unofficially?"

"Some under-something-of-something was nice enough to tell me that he had heard of the hospital. He said it was a reputable place. I got him to call them for me. All they would tell him was that Jake had checked in for treatment but had left long ago."

I sighed. "I'm not surprised."

"You aren't?"

"He was terrified of getting sucked into some system or other," I said.

"Sucked in?"

"He didn't want to start endless treatments that would keep him barely alive, confined to a bed."

Betty snorted. "It isn't as if a dying person gets a lot of choice in the matter." My sister, the stoic, had firm ideas on the subject. To her it was plain as day, a phrase that echoed our mother. "A dying person has an obligation to follow the rules," she said. "He needs to let us nurse him through it." Anything else violated the order of things.

"Jake doesn't see it that way."

That brought Betty up short. "What do you mean? What other way is there to see it?"

That pushed me over the top. "You never understood Jake, but I can't believe you didn't know damn well he had no intention to come back unless he was cured. If he expected to return, he'd have stayed in constant touch. He'd have made arrangements." She scowled, and I decided not to mention that having the disease had reminded Jake of other dreams, reawakened his idea of bliss.

"This won't do," she said.

"What will do? What do you want?"

"You know people there," she said. "Talk to this Ralph person. Find out where Jake is."

"I do know Ralph, but I only met him once. I didn't keep his cell number and can't even remember the company name. I wasn't really that interested. He was Jake's guy."

"Go through Jake's files," she said.

"No need," Doreen said. "I have his number."

We both looked at her. "Why?" I asked.

Surprise crossed her face. "Because I keep Jake's books. I have for years. That's why I know so much about his investments."

"How long has this been going on?"

She laughed at me. "Since he started Campus Cleaners and needed to form a separate company. Who did you think my biggest client is, dummy? I've always kept his books for him."

"You never mentioned it."

"You never asked about my business," she said.

While I stared at my wife, wondering if I really knew her, Betty nudged me. "Call this Ralph. Or just go over there and talk to him. Please. Find out if he knows where Jake went."

"I'll call him," I said.

"I'll book you a flight," Doreen said.

My second trip to Thailand was as uncomfortable and annoying as the first. Being confined with a bunch of other people in a metal tube for 14 hours, plus a five-hour layover in a boring airport in Taipei, provided a constant low level of stress.

During the layover, I noted, however, that there were some cheerful travelers—the ones sitting comfortably in first class. They even had their own lounge. Cattle car provided access to little more than hard plastic chairs and a handful of chain food vendors.

When we re-boarded, passing through the front of the plane, I took in the large seats, the drinks in their hands, I decided it would be worth checking into the cost of upgrading my ticket for my return. Jake could damn well pay for it.

When the plane finally landed in Bangkok, I made the long walk of shame through customs and immigration. Duly processed and stamped, I retrieved my luggage, exiting into the hot streets, heading toward the taxi stand. "Hey Bill!" someone called.

I turned to see Ralph grinning at me. "I was watching for you, mate. Come on along."

"How—?"

"Doreen sent me your flight info, mate. Your missus asked if I'd check to see you arrived and got to your hotel okay."

"Thanks," I said. "I appreciate this." His cheerful and friendly manner made me feel guilty about the image I had of him as a sleazy wheeler dealer.

He grabbed a bag. "Ditch the fucking cart. We can talk in my car."

As soon as he headed out of the parking garage, he looked at me. "I've got some news. While you were snoozing on the plane, I called the embassy, just checking in again. I'm afraid they found Jake's body yesterday."

"Found his body?"

"Washed up on a beach in Pattaya."

"What the hell!"

"They think he died of a drug overdose."

"Jake?"

Ralph shrugged. "Whatever happened, they need you to identify the body. I chatted with Doreen and she faxed over a power of attorney that Betty filled out. Your government still has her listed as his next of kin and we saw no reason to bring up the divorce. The idea is you can ship the body home."

Tall buildings whizzed by along the elevated road adding to my dizziness. "Jake, dead?"

"What happened?" I asked he navigated traffic.

He shook his head. "They aren't sure."

"Why was he in Pattaya? What about the clinic?"

"Ah, yes. Jake came by the day he got to town. We took care of some business and then had a nice dinner. He told me about the shitty luck with the cancer and that he was going to the clinic. They had to run some tests."

"Was he depressed?"

"Not at all, the boy seemed overjoyed to be here. Like he was on vacation, you know." He scowled. "A couple of days later he showed up on my doorstep wanting me to sign a few documents and get some notarized. Said that if anything happened to him, I should give them to you, explain as much of this shit as I understood. Then he had me help him convert some crypto into baht. Quite a bit to be hauling around with him, but that's what he wanted."

"Documents?"

"A bunch of business stuff that he said would wrap things up a bit."

"I need to see them," I said.

"'course. He dodged a small truck as he looked over at me. "Straight to my office then?"

I nodded. "I wouldn't be able to rest now, anyway. The hotel will keep"

His office, situated in an old part of town, in a French colonial building, consisted of a shabby suite of rooms. It seemed smaller than I remembered and had a musty, but not unpleasant smell. His secretary, a lovely Thai girl who looked to be about fourteen, sat in the outer room texting on her phone. She didn't even look up as he led me into the inner office and offered me a drink.

"You'll need this, I imagine."

"It's pretty early."

"Early? Think of it as an obligation," he said. "White man's burden and all that shit. If you like, you can blame it all on Somerset Maugham and that crowd. They made the fucking rules, and it's up to us to live up to their decadent image or there will be hell to pay. It's bad enough we are going to drink whisky. Fail to do even that, and the Minister of Tourism will send thugs over to beat us and force those damn gin and tonics down our throats."

The sarcasm, coming on the heels of learning of Jake's death, seemed inappropriate. Yet, in a dark way, I found it amusing. It lightened the dark cloud over me. I let him ease me into a chair and found myself sipping a surprisingly enjoyable straight whisky.

I found such wicked pleasures intoxicating, I suppose. For me, an early drink was a big step on the wild side.

As I sipped my drink, Ralph opened a desk drawer and pulled out an envelope. He held it up, then pushed it across the table to me. "Here's the deal, Billy." He gave me an evil grin. "It seems your so-called best friend has stuck you with the likes of me."

"How?"

"He signed over his shares in the company to you and Betty—half-half. I can understand doing that to his ex, but I thought you two were mates."

I looked at the documents. "This is half the company."

"Yup. Jake loved the business. After the initial dip, he kept putting in money. Worked out well for the bloke too. Business is over the top. Ever since the US got China up its ass, we've been picking up tons of work from US companies that don't want to get shit from the politicians back home for doing business there. We've got several contracts making toys for big US companies and a lot of inquiries. That's why the Chang Mai operation."

"Are you good with this? With us being involved."

"I ain't interested in buying you out, if that's what you mean. You being my new partners doesn't mean shit in terms of the day-to-day operation. Jake's shares have him as a silent partner. Now we didn't stick to that entirely, but he didn't want to involve himself much, except helping hustle new business."

"So passive income."

"And a right nice cash flow it's become. Your Missus sees that it gets paid out regular too."

"Doreen?"

"She's been auditing the books. Part of Jake's deal." He downed his drink. Then he laughed and waved a paper. "I hadn't noticed this before. Jake left me a little something too."

I looked at it and it was note forgiving Ralph of several thousand dollars for a wager on the dragon-boat races.

Still struggling to accept that Jake was dead, this news rocked me. "I don't understand."

Ralph grinned. "I told your Doreen, and she said he did the same with some other companies, splitting them between you and Betty."

"This is crazy." I was thrashing around, wondering how much Doreen knew. And why?

Ralph grinned and held up the bottle. "Looks like you need a little more chaos conditioner." He refilled my glass.

"What happened to Jake after he left here?"

Ralph shrugged. "Here it is… Jake said that this clinic ran some tests and they found they couldn't treat his condition. He didn't like the options they gave him either. Said they were full of shit about letting him die with dignity. No better than the doctors back home. But once he got the mad out, he grinned and said he had a plan. He knew how to find that. We had a few drinks while my legal guy drew up these papers, and then we signed them."

"So where did he go after that? Where was this place that would let him die with dignity?"

Ralph shrugged. "He didn't say exactly. Since I don't expect to die soon myself, I didn't ask. If it were me, I'd be looking to go out having a good time."

"And you didn't ask where he would go?"

"The man went on about animals crawling off to die so they wouldn't be harassed. Sounded like he was asking to be left alone. We went out for a couple of nights, but he didn't seem inclined to want my company after that. Then he said he was going to get a tan." He opened his hands. "Never saw him again."

"Do you have any idea where I could look for him?"

The man shrugged and refilled the glasses. I hadn't realized mine was empty.

"It's early," I said, not sure what I meant anymore.

"Last time he was over here, I took him down to Pattaya. He took a shine to the place. It's only 100 kilometers down the road. Seeing as they found the body there, I'd guess he went straight there."

"What's there that would draw him?"

"The essentials of life: bars, broads, and gambling."

"But he was sick—dying."

"The lad was a fair way from dead yet, though. Said something about the dignity of a simpler life, basic pleasures and knowing where he could find it."

I thought of Jake's description of bliss, his vision of an idyllic place. "What's the best way to get to Pattaya?"

"Rent a car and driver. The buses are nice, but better to hire a driver for a few days and go exactly when and where you want. I know one who has good English. He can translate for you."

"Thanks."

"What should I tell the embassy?"

"That I have to run some errands. I'll be in touch with them when I get back."

He raised his glass. "That's the spirit. Old Jake ain't going anywhere soon. You have time to chase down all the answers you want." One eyebrow lifted. "It's a good place to have some fun doing it."

"The answers I want?"

"The last thing Jake told me was that Billy boy wouldn't be able to resist following his trail. The idea of you tracking him, wondering about his last days, seemed to amuse him."

I stared at the man. Ralph didn't know Jake well at all, and yet he understood some of what made him tick better than I ever would. Dying was as much a game to Jake as life had been.

As I pondered the idea, this time I was the one who refilled the glasses. "To Jake," I said, raising mine.

"To Jake," he said. "Long may he wave."

"What the fuck does that even mean?"

Ralph laughed. "Not a damn thing, mate. Not a damn thing."

Ralph's stream of non sequiturs was making me dizzy. No, I was getting drunk. And for once, enjoying the feeling. "Long may he wave," I said.

The next morning, Ralph came by in the car he had hired for me. The driver seemed fluent in English, and almost as important, the car had air-conditioning.

"Look, buddy," he told the driver. "This man needs to track down a mate from home. Now, he ain't gonna find him, see, cause he's dead and already in the morgue, but he wants to find out where the bloke went. Take him down to Pattaya so he can poke around."

It seemed to make sense to the driver. I sank down in the back seat. The driver put on some Thai pop music, put the car in gear, and by midday we were in Pattaya. Armed with a recent photo of Jake, we methodically went from hotel to hotel looking for someone who remembered him. No one did.

The area consisted mostly of bars and restaurants, resorts, and guesthouses. There wasn't an obvious location for dignified dying in sight. Even the Buddhist temples seemed garish.

I started to wonder if he'd struck off in a new direction. But he'd ended up here, so it was worth pursuing a bit more.

Late in the afternoon we took a break for a beer and a meal. The burly, tattooed bartender, an Englishman with a friendly grin, seemed to be having a slow day. He asked what we were up to. I told him the whole story—a shortened version, but the story.

The bartender laughed. "Jake, you say? Shit, I know him. Well, a guy named Jake came in here a few times. Had a luscious local gal with him too."

I took out a photo of Jake. "This guy?"

"Yeah, that's him. A lot more pale and hollowed cheeks, but that's him."

"Do you know where he was staying?"

The bartender laughed. "That's one reason I remember him. He mentioned that he had found heaven over at the Pattaya Palace. That's not exactly a hot spot and I asked him why not stick around here, closer to the action? We had plenty of rooms and we are in the middle of all the vices known to man. He said he needed a little peace. Said he came here to die."

"That's right."

"No shit? I'm afraid that when he started a little sermonette about dying with dignity, I went off to serve other customers. People spin all sorts of stories in here. I thought he might be after free drinks." He paused. "If your pal really was dying, I got to admit the Pattaya Palace ain't a bad choice for that sort of thing. Perfect for going out quiet like."

"I know this place," my driver said. "It not very high-end."

"What do you mean?" I asked.

The bartender laughed. "He means it's an old school beach place—bungalows, kind of quiet. Even the bar is mellow. The locals don't get why foreigners would stay there. Still, there are some fine girls, good booze, and a nice beach. It's just a bit low on parties and discos for most people" He grinned. "But I guess a man banging a sexy local girl wouldn't need our parties."

"I'll check it out."

"Pierre, a French kid, owns the place. I think his Daddy bought it for him to keep him out of France for a while."

I paid the tab, tipping well, then we headed off. My pulse raced. Finally, I felt that I was getting close to real answers.

We found Pierre behind the reception desk drinking anise. A friendly sort, he poured me one and happily admitted to knowing Jake. "Terrific guy," he said.

"And he stayed here?"

"He and the girl. He bought one of the beach bungalows."

"Bought it?"

"Yeah. My Papa would kill me if he knew. They are supposed to be rentals, but he fell in love with the place. When he offered me more than it was worth, I had to sell it to him. It's been a slow year. Too bad he only owned it for a week or so before he died. Too bad he died."

"Yes."

"I'm the one who found him."

"On the beach?"

"Yeah. I told the girl, but she already knew. She gave me his passport and written instructions telling me to call the embassy. He didn't want her involved."

"What happens to the bungalow now?"

The man shrugged. "Nothing. He put it in the girl's name." I must've been giving him the open-mouthed stupid look because he laughed. "She's there now, I think." He pointed at a thatched roof hut on the beach. "That one."

I bought beers for the driver and myself, and one for the Frenchman too. Then, with my stomach in a knot, I walked across the sand toward the bungalow to meet this girlfriend. I was trying to picture that. Jake with a Thai girlfriend? And he'd bought her a bungalow?

A slim young Thai woman was sitting on the porch staring out to sea. "Hello," I said.

"You want massage?" she asked, sounding hopeful.

I looked her over and guessed she was in her twenties. She wasn't beautiful, but pleasant enough, with small firm breasts under a thin tee shirt; her shorts showed lovely brown legs.

"A massage?"

She pointed to a sign. "Oil massage 500 Baht."

"No, I was hoping to talk to you about Jake."

"Jake?"

"The man who bought this bungalow."

"Nice man," she said.

"Why did he do that? Buy you a bungalow?"

Her look told me that she had little respect for my ability to grasp the obvious. "So I not have to pay rent. I keep more money from massages."

"Did you ask him to do that?"

She got up, moving catlike toward me, before stopping to put her hands on her hips and look me over. "You are Billy Boy," she said.

"How did you know?"

"Jake tell me. He say, 'After I die, Billy Boy come see you and ask too many questions."

That sounded exactly like something Jake would say. "I only ask because I'm trying to understand."

"Understand what?"

"Why did he come here in the first place?"

She laughed. "To get a massage." Then she smiled. "The first time he come to get a massage. Every day a massage. The second time he come back to see me. The last time he come here to be happy and have someone take care of him."

"Take care of him? Are you a nurse?"

She laughed. "No. He not want a nurse or a doctor." Her smiled was delightful. "Jake a smart man. He say a dying man just needs a woman who can make the last days good and beautiful. He ask if I can be nice to him, make love to him when he like, while he can."

"And you agreed."

She stood and motioned for me to follow her. "I show."

An onshore breeze wafted across the open porch and the bungalow had double doors front and back to welcome it. I followed the girl as she moved through the doors as if she floated on the breeze. I drifted in the wake of this insubstantial waif who led me to the seaside where a hammock was strung.

"He like to lie there and look out at water."

The hammock was perfectly positioned to give a man a clear view of the Gulf of Thailand. I imagined Jake there, content. "At first, we just live together, being happy. I fix him good Thai food and bring him whisky in his hammock."

"At first."

She shrugged. "His pain grew bad, so bad that massages, good sex no longer enough to wash it away. I brought him opium to smoke. He like for a time." She made a face. "He had me get other drugs too, but these we put away. For later. He said he wanted to be clear when he meet death."

"Clear?"

"Too many drugs, the ones that took away all the pain, he didn't like. He think they are not a dignified way to wait for death. He want to meet death face-to-face and talk plain."

"And yet, he died of an overdose."

She nodded. "One night he wake me. 'Death came for a chat,' he said. 'We had a long talk and settled things, walking along the beach.' He was ready."

"He settled things with death?"

"Enough."

"I don't understand."

"He had me get the drugs. We walked in the full moonlight to the edge of the water. We lie on a blanket on the edge of the water. It made a gentle sound. I watched him take many drugs—all of them. Then we made love."

"What happened next?"

"He slept. When the sun began to rise, I said goodbye. The Gulf has small tides, the water doesn't come up far, but we were close to it already. Slowly the sea come in I watched it wash him away."

I could picture it. It sounded oddly peaceful, serene. "Yes."

"The next day I tell Pierre that someone find him soon, give him the papers Jake left."

"He mentioned that."

"You want the money now?"

"What money?"

She led me inside to an ancient, intricately carved desk. On it was a carved box fashioned out of some dark wood. I opened it to find it filled with Thai money. While I stared at it, she opened a drawer and took out some documents. "Jake said to show you this. Billy boy will need some of these papers, he said."

When I started reading, my knees grew weak. I sat on the bed, and the girl sat next to me, her body radiating a sensual heat.

The top sheet was a note. "Hey, Billy boy," he wrote, "I'm sure you've been told that I offed myself. That means the insurance company will probably raise hell about paying out. Naturally, Betty is my beneficiary and see if you can't make them cough it up. If not, don't worry. I left her plenty of money and there is a brokerage account with stocks and bonds that is in her name. Doreen knows how to access it.

"The cash in this box is for the lovely girl you've met by now. She was a blessing and deserves every baht and the bungalow too. You should already have the shares in Ralph's company now—you and Betty deserve that too. Let Ralph do his thing and rake in the money.

"I hope you can see with your own eyes that, despite all odds, and Robert Frost, I managed to travel both roads, even if the one less traveled was a tad shorter than I might have liked. Boy, was I lucky. Who the hell gets to do that? Take care, buddy, and I'll see you on the other side one day."

The girl walked up and handed me a cold bottle of beer. I drank thirstily, then I handed her the money. "He wanted you to have this."

Without a flicker of emotion, she put it back in the box and replaced it on the desk. I looked away. The touch of her slight hand, slender fingers on my arm made me turn back. A delicious, delicate, and erotic contact that made me tremble. I looked down at her face and saw a lovely, seductive smile—a smile could change how a man saw the world. "Jake was a nice man," she said. "I miss him."

"Did you love him?"

She shook her head. "I made love with him. I made him feel loved."

It all made a certain amount of sense. There were still blanks, but none this girl could fill in. She had played her role in Jake's exit.

"I should go," I said.

The girl cocked her head. "You could stay. With me. Your friend Jake would not mind."

In that moment, a desire for this creature rippled through me. I swallowed, knowing that if I stayed another hour, I would stay the night. And if I spent the night, I might never leave.

This, then, was the attraction Jake must have felt, the allure that drew him back. I didn't have half his strength. And while this road of Jake's, and the girl he'd followed down it both called to my primal being, I still was traveling another path.

"I must go. My family needs me and to know what happened to Jake. And I have a car waiting."

She stood up, smiling, nodding.

As I turned to go, I saw a copy of the brochure for the clinic sitting on the table. Someone had used a felt-tip pen to underline the phase that meant so much to Jake: death with dignity. Whatever that meant to Jake, apparently, he found it.

At the door, I stopped and gave the girl one last look. She smiled. "I didn't ask your name," he said. "That was rude."

She laughed. "Your thoughts were about your friend, not me. He was important to you."

"More important than I knew."

"And you were important to him."

"Why do you say that?"

"One reason he needed me was that he wasn't strong enough to be around you or his family in his last days. He couldn't stand the idea that you would all be angry with him for not being willing to do anything that would keep him alive a few extra days or weeks."

"He wanted to die with dignity," I said.

"Yes," she said, giving me an enchanting smile that made my heart pound. For a moment, I considered the possibility that she might be attracted to me. That was crazy, of course. I couldn't stay here. I had a wife, children, and business to run. This wasn't even my dream. It was Jake's. I wouldn't be out of his influence for a long time. "Still," I said. "It was rude not to ask. You were trying to help my best friend. I should know your name."

She turned her head and stared out across the Gulf of Thailand for a moment. "My name... Jake couldn't say it in Thai, so he always called me Dignity."

When I returned to Bangkok, Ralph took me to the embassy where I arranged for Jake's last international flight. We talked about things and had dinner and then talked some more. I'd developed an appreciation for the man, and he declared that I was 'loosening up nicely.' High praise in Australia, I assumed.

A few days later, I flew back to the US— traveling first class, just as I'd promised myself. From the moment I boarded, I wondered why the hell I hadn't done it before. What a difference there was.

The seats, the service, the food, the VIP lounge in Taipei… everything was amazing.

It seemed odd that I didn't understand the true value of comfort until now. In roundabout ways, Jake's death was teaching me a lot about life.

"You look refreshed," Doreen said when she picked me up at the airport.

"In more ways that you can know," I said. "How is Betty?"

"Reconciled," she said. "She is such a stoic that she could accept the idea that Jake deliberately overdosed on pain pills after the treatments at the clinic failed."

"Good."

"I think the news that Jake left her a wealthy woman was the bigger shock." Then she hit me with that devastatingly amused, sly smile. "Are you going to tell me what really happened?"

There was no point in pretending, and I wanted to talk about it. I told her the whole story. "I'm still digesting it all. I'm not sure I should tell Betty all of it."

"Jake wanted his dignity. She gains nothing by hearing a story she won't like or understand," Doreen said. "And telling the truth, the whole truth, and nothing but the truth is highly overrated. Worst of all, she won't even get the joke."

I let out a sigh. "True enough."

It was also true that the story didn't seem to surprise my wife... well, that didn't surprise me. Not anymore.

"Seems you had a much bigger hand in Jake's businesses than I ever knew."

She grinned. "Jake couldn't do it on his own."

"And you didn't think to tell me?"

She looked at me. "And give you a chance to object? That would have been... undignified."

"I suppose it would have been."

"Can't have that," she said.

"I'm just learning who you are," I said.

I couldn't fathom the smile she gave me. "And how do you like me so far?"

I laughed. "Pretty damn well. It's sexy."

"You are changing," she said.

"I've been told I'm loosing up nicely. And that came from an expert. Do you agree?"

"Is there any question? You flying first class? Lying to Betty?"

"I suppose I am. Jake left a void. Not one that I want to fill exactly. But I've learned that he's been propping me up. His death meant I had to change."

"Or fall over," she said.

"How do you like me so far?" I asked.

She wrinkled her nose. "You are still upright, so I'll call it a work in progress. But you show promise."

"On the way back here, with all that time on the plane and sitting in airports to fill up, I did a lot of thinking. Jake gave me a lot to think about and some of it… well, I have some ideas."

"I like ideas," she said.

"I talked a lot with Ralph."

"Sleazy Ralph? Do tell."

"I deserve that. Anyway, he was talking about opportunities to expand the manufacturing business."

"More?"

"By opening facilities in Vietnam."

"Halfway around the world?"

"They have a good, well-trained workforce."

"Okay, Billy boy, now I'm waiting for the punchline."

"Well, he is busy with the new operation in Chang Mai. He is complaining that even he can't be everywhere at once."

"That tends to be difficult even for Australians. So what does that mean to you?"

"To us. This fall the youngest starts college."

"I just got the bill for the tuition and the dorm."

"What would you think about moving to Asia?"

"What about the business here?"

"I'm tired of the cleaning business. Do you think we could turn it over to Betty?"

"Betty is thriving. She's been fretting about what she'd do when you came back. She is enjoying being in charge. And our new big client thinks she is great."

"Then maybe we should make her CEO."

"Are you sure?"

"I need to make my mark on something. I've spent my life running something Jake started. Now, he got us into this business too, but I'd be tackling new things."

She pursed her lips. "Starting up new operations in a new country would require a huge learning curve."

"That part I do well," I said.

"And it will take a long time," she said. "We'd either have to lease our house or sell it."

"We should sell it," I told her.

"You are being impulsive and imprudent, Billy Boy."

"If I keep being impulsive and imprudent, will you go back to calling me Bill?"

"Deal."

"If we are going to do this, let's cut all the ties we can. We will want to keep our options open over there. Happily, for once, we don't need to worry about cash flow."

"My," she said. "Whatever you found following Jake's trail seems to have inspired you. Care to share?"

"Things came together. And then the whole idea of dying with dignity... I met her."

That earned me a huge grin. "So you said. What's she like?"

"It's what she represented to Jake. Simple, primitive, basic."

"And he needed to die with dignity," she said. "Is she pretty?"

"Not as pretty as you."

"Right answer." She took my arm. "Here's the deal, darling. If we go over there, to Vietnam, or wherever, you have to promise you won't be dying with dignity any time soon."

"You wouldn't be supportive? It's a noble goal."

"Well, someday, perhaps. But you said you were just learning who I really was."

"I think that more all the time."

"Then before we even get to any chat about dying with dignity, I expect you focus on living with whoever Doreen turns out to be."

"Deal, partner," I said.

THE END

"I shall be telling this with a sigh
Somewhere ages and ages hence:
Two roads diverged in a wood, and I—
I took the one less traveled by,
And that has made all the difference."
— Robert Frost

ABOUT THE AUTHORS

J. LEE PORTER

J. Lee Porter is a former IT specialist, programmer, and data analyst for banking, security, and government agencies. He left the IT world behind on July 4, 2016, declaring it his personal Independence Day to travel the world full time in search of inspiration for his writing.

Jeff is on Twitter at @JLPorterAuthor
His website is http://www.nomadicgiant.com

ED TEJA

Ed Teja is a writer, poet, musician, and boat bum. He writes about the places he knows and the people who live in the margins of the world. After being friends with tech giants, pirates, fishermen, and a coterie of strange people for many years, he finds the world an amazing place filled with intriguing, if sometimes crazed, characters.

You can contact Ed on Twitter at @ETeja
His website is www.edteja.com

If you liked this story, please leave a review.
And check out their Bitpat Series of
political/techothrillers
on Amazon

www.ingramcontent.com/pod-product-compliance
Lightning Source LLC
Chambersburg PA
CBHW060943120626
46557CB00003B/1124